Let's Play a Hockey Game!

Kari-Lynn Winters

illustrated by
Helen Flook

North Winds Press
An Imprint of Scholastic Canada Ltd.

The artwork is drawn and painted in FW acrylic inks, enhanced here and there with
Caran d'Ache coloured pencils on non-surface hot-pressed 50% cotton Fabriano paper.

Library and Archives Canada Cataloguing in Publication
Winters, Kari-Lynn, 1969-, author
Let's play a hockey game! / Kari-Lynn Winters ; illustrated
by Helen Flook.

Story in rhyme.
ISBN 978-1-4431-4818-4 (hardback)

1. Children's poetry, Canadian (English). I. Flook, Helen,
illustrator II. Title.

PS8645.I5745L48 2016   jC811'.6   C2016-901622-6

www.scholastic.ca

6 5 4 3 2 1   Printed in Malaysia 108   16 17 18 19 20

To Chris, Ken, Patricia and Scot for your assists with the words and for helping me score this book. And a callout to Jase, Cooper and Mel — three all-star readers and hockey fans.

— K.W.

For Roland and Macsen, my two favourite hockey players.

— H.F.

Time to play:
It's hockey guess time!
To score a goal, call out the rhyme.

The buzzer blares.
Are you set?

Slap the shot.
It's an open . . .

5

ONE goal scored — a point for you!
Guess again. Make it **TWO.**

This chilly space (what do you think?)

It's icy.
It's oval.
It's called a . . .

RINK!

8

Against the boards, don't get stuck.
It's black. It's round.
Backhand that . . .

9

PUCK!

Awesome aim! That makes **THREE.**
You know a lot about

HOOOOC—KEY!

A rocket shot. You're so slick.
Slap that puck with your hockey . . .

STICK!

Another score!
You've got **FOUR**.
Stay alive.
Try for **FIVE!**

Interference — watch those blocks!
Don't end up in the
penalty . . .

BOX!

Seconds left.
A clash of sticks.
Into the net, make it **SIX!**

At the drop, try not to cough.
You want to win
the face . . .

OFF!

22

The coach gives the hat trick sign.
Three more goals . . . **SEVEN,
EIGHT, NINE.**

Oooh, this game is really great.
I like the way you stop and . . . **SKATE!**

Oooh, this game is really fine.
Move the puck past the centre . . .
LINE!

Oooh, this game is really tense.
I like the way you play **DEEE . . . FENCE!**

A breakaway once again.
Slam the shot. Shoot for **TEN!**

Pass the puck — a five hole!
Between her skates,
another . . .

GOAL!

The crowd goes wild!
Team play, you see!
You know a lot about . . .

HOOOOC—KEY!